The Wild Pony

Do you love ponies? Be a Pony Pal!

Look for these Pony Pal books:

#1   I Want a Pony

#2   A Pony for Keeps

#3   A Pony in Trouble

#4   Give Me Back My Pony

#5   Pony to the Rescue

#6   Too Many Ponies

#7   Runaway Pony

#8   Good-bye Pony

coming soon

Super Special #1   The Baby Pony

PONY PALS®

The Wild Pony

Jeanne Betancourt

illustrated by Paul Bachem

A
LITTLE APPLE
PAPERBACK

SCHOLASTIC INC.
New York Toronto London Auckland Sydney

No part of this publication may be reproduced in whole or in part, or stored in a retrieval system, or transmitted in any form or by any means, electronic, mechanical, photocopying, recording, or otherwise, without written permission of the publisher. For information regarding permission, write to Scholastic Inc., 555 Broadway, New York, NY 10012.

ISBN 0-590-62974-3

Text copyright © 1996 by Jeanne Betancourt.
Illustrations copyright © 1996 by Scholastic Inc.
All rights reserved. Published by Scholastic Inc.
APPLE PAPERBACKS® and the APPLE PAPERBACKS® logo are registered trademarks of Scholastic Inc.

12 11 10   9/9 0 1/0

Printed in the U.S.A.   40

First Scholastic printing, March 1996

With thanks to Margaret Barney, Shanna Barney, and Linda Brink.

Contents

The Wild Pony

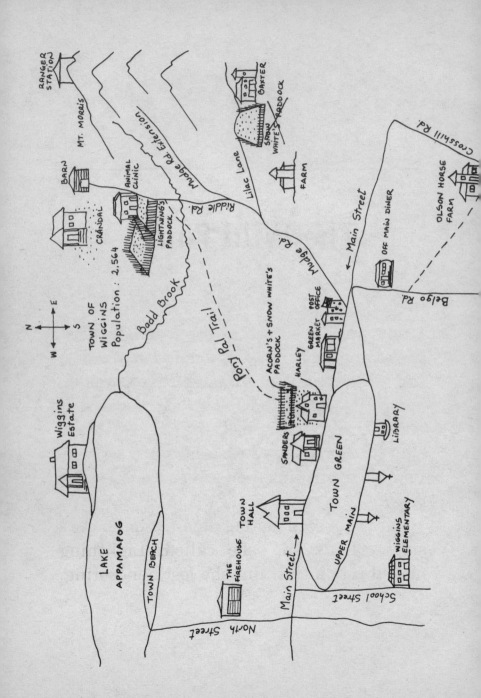

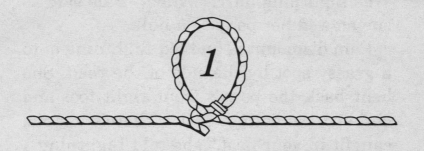

A Cry for Help

Pam Crandal smiled as she rode her pony, Lightning, down Mudge Road. It was a sunny Saturday morning and Pam was on her way to meet her Pony Pals, Anna and Lulu. They were meeting at Off-Main Diner for breakfast before a long trail ride. Pam loved riding her sweet Connemara pony.

Pam squeezed her legs against her pony's sides. "Let's go," she called. Lightning moved into a trot. But she lost her footing.

Was Lightning hurt? "Whoa," Pam said as she slowed her pony to a halt.

Pam dismounted and led Lightning onto a grassy spot by the side of the road. She bent back the pony's front right foot and checked the bottom of it. "There's a stone caught in your hoof," she told Lightning.

Pam took a hoof pick out of her saddlebag and used it to dig out the stone. She was putting the pick away when Lightning tossed her head and whinnied. Pam heard a distant whinny answering her pony's call. She looked in the direction of the sound. Was there a pony standing at the far end of the field? Pam moved closer to the fence for a better view. It *was* a pony. "Hi, there!" Pam called to the pony.

The pony turned and disappeared into a row of bushes. Whose pony was that? Pam wondered.

She heard the *clip-clop* of horses' hooves on the road. She saw her friends, Anna and Lulu, riding their ponies toward her. Pam waved. Lightning bobbed her head a few times as if to say hello to the ponies, Snow White and Acorn.

Lulu and Anna halted near Pam and Lightning.

"How come you're not riding?" asked Anna.

"Is Lightning okay?" asked Lulu.

Pam told her friends about the stone in Lightning's hoof. Then she told them about the pony she had just seen. "It's so strange seeing a pony here," Pam said.

"What's so strange about seeing a pony?" asked Anna. "Lots of people have ponies around here."

Pam pointed to a FOR SALE sign stuck in the ground a few yards from them. "This place is for sale," she said. "No one lives here."

"People sell their houses while they're still living in them," said Anna.

"But the man who lived here moved away," said Pam.

"Maybe someone else moved in," said Lulu.

3

"I'd know it if they did," Pam said. "I go by here all the time. Besides, the sign's still here."

"Maybe it's a lost pony," said Lulu.

"Then we should go look for it," suggested Pam.

Anna and Lulu agreed that the Pony Pals should look for the pony. "I'll stay here with our ponies," said Anna. "You go search for the pony."

Pam and Lulu crawled under the fence. "Which way did the pony go?" asked Lulu.

Pam pointed across the field. "Into those bushes," she said.

Pam and Lulu walked along the edge of the field. "What did the pony look like?" asked Lulu.

"I didn't get a good look," said Pam. "I just noticed it was a pony and brown."

The two girls found a path through the bushes and came out in another field. But the pony wasn't there, either. Beyond the field they saw a big brick house with a paddock. The pony wasn't in the paddock.

"Let's go see if it's on the other side of the house," suggested Lulu. Pam and Lulu tiptoed around the brick house. When they got to the other side, they saw the pony. It was drinking from a stream. The two girls stood still and watched.

Seeing the pony made Pam so sad she wanted to cry. It was a mare whose coat was covered in mud. Her tail was knotted with burrs. Worst of all, she was the skinniest pony Pam had ever seen.

"No one's been taking care of her," whispered Lulu.

Pam nodded. She knew Lulu felt sad, too. "The poor pony," Pam said.

The pony backed up from the stream and nuzzled the ground. It was early spring and the grass had hardly grown. Pam wondered how long it had been since the pony had hay and oats to eat. She wished she had some oats with her.

Suddenly the pony raised her head and sniffed the wind. Then she whipped around and galloped into the woods.

"She smelled us," said Pam.

"Let's follow her," said Lulu.

"No," said Pam. "She's afraid of us. We don't want to scare her. Besides, there are No Trespassing signs all over this place."

"But we've got to help her," said Lulu. "She looks awful."

"I know," said Pam. "Let's go tell Anna we saw the pony. Then we'll all decide what to do next."

Pam and Lulu peeked into the windows of the brick house. There was no furniture inside. "You're right, Pam," said Lulu. "No one's living here."

"And no one is taking care of that pony," said Pam.

Back on Mudge Road, Pam and Lulu told Anna all about the pony.

"It sounds like she's a wild pony," said Anna.

Lulu and Pam agreed. "We need to find out who the wild pony belongs to," said Lulu.

"Let's go to the diner and have a Pony Pal meeting," said Pam.

Pam rubbed the white upside-down heart on Lightning's forehead. She wondered about the wild pony. Was she lost? Was there a girl or boy somewhere in Wiggins wondering what had happened to their pony?

Wild Pony

The Pony Pals rode down Mudge Road toward town. "That poor pony," said Lulu. "I hope we can help her."

"Me too," said Pam. Pam knew that Lulu Sanders was the perfect person to help the wild pony. Lulu's father studied and wrote about wild animals. Lulu's mother died when she was little, so Lulu used to travel with her father and help him with his assignments. Now she was living with her grandmother in Wiggins. Pam knew that Lulu missed her father and was sad that she didn't have a mother. But Lulu was happy in Wiggins and a great Pony Pal.

Lulu's grandmother's house was right next door to Anna's house. Snow White and Acorn shared the paddock behind the two houses. And that paddock was connected to Lightning's paddock by a mile-and-a-half trail that cut through the woods. The Pony Pals called it Pony Pal Trail.

Lulu was new to Wiggins, but Pam and Anna had lived in Wiggins all their lives. Pam Crandal and Anna Harley had been best friends since kindergarten. Anna was dyslexic, so it was difficult for her to learn reading and math. But she was very smart, a terrific artist, and always had fun ideas.

Pam liked school and got A's in every subject. And she liked having fun as much as Lulu and Anna. Most of all, the three friends loved ponies. Pam's father was a veterinarian and her mother was a riding teacher. Pam had owned a pony for as long as she could remember.

The Pony Pals halted their ponies in

front of Off-Main Diner. They tied them to the hitching post and went in. Anna's mother ran the diner, so the Pony Pals always felt right at home there. "You get our drinks," Anna told Pam and Lulu, "and I'll tell Cook our order."

A few minutes later the three girls were sitting in their favorite booth, eating blueberry pancakes and talking about the wild pony.

"I bet she was out all winter," said Pam.

"All by herself and with hardly anything to eat," said Lulu.

"It's so cruel to leave a pony without food," added Anna. "We've got to help her."

"I wish we knew who owns the pony," said Pam.

"The property is for sale," Lulu said. "So a real estate agent might know something about the pony."

"Let's go next door and ask Mrs. Baxter," said Anna.

The girls finished eating their breakfast, cleared the table, and left the diner. Pam was glad to see that Mrs. Baxter was sitting at the big desk near the window of the real estate office. The Pony Pals didn't like *Mr.* Baxter. He was grumpy. But Mrs. Baxter was always happy to see them. When they walked into the office, she looked up and said, "Hi, girls. It's nice to see you. What's up?"

"We have a question about the big property that's for sale on Mudge Road," Pam said.

Mrs. Baxter smiled and asked, "Do you want to buy it?"

The girls laughed and said no. "We saw a pony there," Pam said.

"She looked awfully skinny," said Lulu.

"No one's been taking care of her," added Anna.

"We wondered if you knew anything about it," said Pam.

"The property is owned by Amos Kennedy," Mrs. Baxter said. "But he moved to

California before the winter. Mr. Kennedy didn't say anything to me about a pony."

"Maybe he left her behind," said Lulu. "It could cost a lot of money to trailer a pony from Connecticut to California."

"If he left a pony," said Mrs. Baxter, "I think he would have asked someone to look after it."

"No one's been looking after this pony," said Pam sadly.

"Maybe the pony came from another property and is lost," said Mrs. Baxter.

"Ponies have a great sense of direction," said Pam. "They don't get lost so easily."

Mrs. Baxter looked at her watch. "I have to meet a client in a few minutes," she said. "I'm sorry I can't help you girls more right now. Let me know if you see that pony on the property again. Then I'll get in touch with Mr. Kennedy and ask him about it."

The Pony Pals said good-bye to Mrs. Baxter and went outside. "Let's go back and look for the pony now," said Anna.

14

"This time we'll bring oats with us when we track her," said Lulu.

"I don't know," said Pam. "There were No Trespassing signs all over that place."

"Mrs. Baxter said to let her know if we see the pony again," said Anna. "That's like giving us permission."

"Okay," Pam said.

The girls mounted their ponies and headed back toward Mudge Road. "What if we can't find her?" said Anna. "She might be hiding on us."

"I bet she'll come out to see our ponies," said Lulu. "Ponies are herd animals. They love being together."

When the Pony Pals reached Mr. Kennedy's property they rode up the driveway and put their ponies in the paddock next to the house.

"How will the wild pony know that our ponies are here?" asked Pam.

"If she hears them whinnying, I bet she'll come running out," said Lulu.

Anna pushed her fingers through Acorn's

mane. "Come on, Acorn," she said. "Give me a big whinny." Acorn didn't make a sound.

Lulu looked her pony straight in the eye and made a soft whinny sound. Snow White answered her with a happy nicker. Then Acorn whinnied at Snow White. And Lightning whinnied at both of them.

The Pony Pals stood in the middle of the paddock and waited. But the wild pony didn't appear.

"Why isn't it working?" asked Lulu.

"Remember, she's afraid of people," said Anna.

"If she thinks we left, maybe she'll come to be with our ponies," said Pam. "Let's hide."

"Good idea," said Lulu. She pointed to a clump of bushes in a corner of the field. "There's a good hiding spot."

The girls crouched behind the bushes. "I wonder how long we'll have to wait?" whispered Anna.

"Once my father sat behind a rock

twenty-four hours to see a gorilla," Lulu said.

Pam didn't care how long she had to wait. She was going to do everything she could to help the wild pony.

Hide-and-Seek

The Pony Pals waited behind the bushes for the wild pony to come out of hiding.

After a while Lulu whispered, "I think I see her. She's coming out of the woods."

Pam peered through the branches. The wild pony was walking slowly across the field toward the paddock. "Look how skinny she is," said Anna. "She must be starving."

Acorn looked up, saw the strange pony, and went back to dozing. Snow White watched the pony for a few seconds and went back to searching for grass in the mud. But when Lightning saw the pony at the fence, she nickered softly and trotted toward her. The two ponies began sniffing each other's faces.

"Uh-oh," said Pam. "I shouldn't let Lightning be so close to her. What if she has a disease? Lightning could catch it."

"She might have strangles," said Lulu. "Ponies can catch that disease easily."

"I'm going to put some oats out in the field," said Pam. "Maybe that will distract her from Lightning."

"Be careful not to scare her," said Lulu.

Pam walked quietly into the field. She emptied a small bag of oats on a flat rock in the middle of the field. The wild pony didn't notice her. But when Lightning saw Pam she nickered as if to say, "Hey, bring those oats here." Pam froze like a statue. The wild pony noticed her and sniffed the air. Pam knew that the pony was deciding whether to run away from her or move toward the oats. Pam returned to the hiding place. The Pony Pals watched

to see what would happen next.

The wild pony sniffed the air again. Then she rushed to the small pile of oats on the rock. The Pony Pals smiled at one another and hit silent high five's. When the pony finished the oats, she looked around as if to say, "Give me some more."

"I have some oats in my backpack," whispered Lulu.

"She shouldn't have any more oats now," said Pam. "Horses have small stomachs. She could get sick from too much food."

"I have an apple," said Anna. "It's small. Can she have that?"

"Okay," said Pam.

"Pam, you bring it to her," Anna said. "She's getting used to you." Anna gave Pam the apple.

Pam walked to the rock, holding the apple out in front of her. "Here, pony," she said in a gentle voice. "Here's an apple for you."

When the pony saw Pam, she tossed her head back as if she might run away. Pam held the apple out in front of her. The pony stayed. She took a small step toward Pam. Pam took a small step toward the pony. The pony took another step. Pam took another step. Suddenly the pony trotted up to Pam, took the apple, and stepped back to eat it. When she finished, the pony looked at Pam to see if she had more apples. "You're a good pony," said Pam. She reached out to pat the pony's cheek. The pony suddenly turned and galloped across the field into the woods. Lightning whinnied after her, but the pony did not turn back.

Anna and Lulu came out of hiding. "What happened?" asked Lulu.

"I frightened her," said Pam. "She didn't want me to touch her."

"How can we help her if we can't touch her?" asked Anna.

"At least we can feed her," said Lulu. "Tomorrow, let's bring her some hay."

"And grooming supplies," said Anna, "in case she lets us touch her."

"I think she has a black coat under all the mud," said Pam.

The three friends sat on the flat rock and made a list of what they needed to take care of the pony.

For the wild pony

- Oats for two small feedings
- Vitamin powder
- Lots of hay
- 2 Currycombs
- 2 Hard brushes
- 2 Soft brushes
- Rub rag
- Scissors
- Hoof pick
- Apples and carrots

After dinner that night, Pam told her parents about the wild pony. "Did you ever take care of a pony for Mr. Kennedy?" Pam asked her father.

"I gave shots to a sweet black pony for Mr. Kennedy a year or so back," said Dr. Crandal. "That's the only time he called me."

"So it *is* Mr. Kennedy's pony!" said Pam. "He moved away and left his pony alone."

"Then that poor pony was alone all winter," said Pam's mother. "How terrible for her."

"Can I bring her here?" asked Pam. "I promise I'll be responsible for her."

"It's not your pony to take," said Mrs. Crandal. "It's Mr. Kennedy's pony. It's his property."

"Mr. Kennedy doesn't even care about her," said Pam. "He left her all alone all winter. Please say we can bring her here."

"Maybe Mr. Kennedy thought someone was looking after the pony," said Mrs.

Crandal. "And that person didn't do their job."

"Maybe," agreed Pam.

"The best thing you can do for the pony is to tell Mrs. Baxter you saw her again," said Dr. Crandal.

Pam thought about the skinny black pony covered in mud and burrs. She remembered the hungry way the pony gobbled up the apple. Until Mr. Kennedy decided what to do with his pony, Pam knew she had to take care of her.

Beauty

The next morning the Pony Pals met at the FOR SALE sign on the Kennedy property. Pam's backpack was stuffed with hay for the pony.

"I brought the oats, an apple, and some carrots," said Lulu.

"And I've got the grooming supplies," Anna said.

The three girls went up the driveway and around to the back of the house. "There she is," whispered Lulu, "near the stream."

Just then the pony looked up and saw them. She ran into the woods.

"Why is she so afraid of people?" said Lulu.

"Something must have happened to her," Pam said. "My dad said she was a sweet pony when he gave her shots."

"She was alone all winter," said Lulu. "Maybe she doesn't trust people anymore."

"Or maybe that's just the way she is," said Anna, "and that's why Mr. Kennedy left her."

The Pony Pals went over to the flat rock in the field. Lulu put out half a handful of oats. Anna mixed in a teaspoon of vitamin powder. Pam laid down hay a few feet away. Then the three friends went over to the edge of the field and sat on the ground to wait for the pony.

After a few minutes, the pony came out of the woods and trotted over to the flat rock. "She knew where to go for oats," said Anna. "She's so smart."

The pony gobbled up the oats, then looked around. "I think she's looking for an apple," whispered Anna. Lulu handed Pam an apple.

Pam stood up and walked slowly toward the pony. The pony trotted up to Pam, reached with her neck, and lifted the apple out of Pam's hand. Then Anna came up beside Pam and held out a handful of hay. The pony looked suspiciously at Anna.

"It's okay," Pam told the pony. "Anna's your friend, too." The pony snatched up the hay and backed up to eat it.

"I'm going to try to touch her," Pam whispered. Pam walked around to the pony's side. "Good pony," she said. She touched the pony's side gently, and for only a second. The pony gave a little jump. But she didn't run away. Pam touched the pony's side again. This time the pony wasn't surprised. She touched the pony a few more times. Each time Pam left her hand on the pony's side a little longer.

Anna handed a currycomb to Pam. Pam

ran the comb in circles over a small section of the pony's coat. A hunk of dried mud fell to the ground and a cloud of dirt blew in Pam's face. Pam continued working. The pony nickered softly. "I think she likes it," Lulu whispered. Pam worked the curry-comb over larger and larger areas of the pony's side. More dried mud fell to the ground. More dust blew up around Pam. But Pam didn't mind. She was taking care of the wild pony.

"I'm going to try the other side," said Anna. Anna made sure the pony was used to her touch before she used the curry-comb.

The pony nickered again as if to say, "This feels good."

The Pony Pals smiled at one another. The wild pony was getting used to them.

Now Lulu brushed the parts Pam and Anna had already curried. "I bet she'll look beautiful when the mud and her winter coat are gone," said Lulu.

"Maybe she's *all* black," said Anna.

"If we keep putting vitamins in her oats, her coat will really shine," said Pam. She reached out to stroke the pony's cheek. The pony shook her head and jumped away.

"She doesn't like to be touched on the head," said Lulu.

"How will we get the burrs out of her mane if she won't let us touch her head?" asked Anna.

"She'll let us do it when she trusts us more," said Pam.

The girls were concentrating on their work and didn't see the man coming up behind them. "This pony doesn't look wild to me," he said.

The girls looked up, and the pony jerked her head around at the sound of the voice. It was Pam's father. She was glad to see that he had his medical bag with him.

"How's she doing?" Dr. Crandal asked the girls.

"She's a little jittery," Lulu answered.

"And she doesn't want anyone to touch her head," said Pam.

"But she's a sweet pony," added Anna. "And she's getting used to us."

"Well, let's take a look at you," Dr. Crandal said to the pony. He was careful not to touch the pony's face, but he still looked at her eyes, nose, and ears. Then he listened to her heart and lungs and felt her leg muscles. When he finished examining the pony, Dr. Crandal told the girls, "She's undernourished and her coat is a mess, but otherwise she looks okay. I checked my record. Mr. Kennedy has a nine-year-old black Morgan. I'd say this is the same pony."

"Dad, if you have a record on the pony you must know her name," said Pam.

Dr. Crandal looked at the skinny, still-dirty pony. "It's not a name that suits her very well right now," he said.

"What is it?" asked Lulu.

"Her name is Beauty," he said.

"*Beauty!*" exclaimed Anna. "That's a perfect name for her. She's beautiful under all that mud, Dr. Crandal. You'll see."

"She just needs someone to take care of her," said Lulu. "She was alone all winter."

"Poor Beauty," said Pam. She reached up to pat the pony on the head. Beauty jerked her head back, galloped across the field, and disappeared into the woods.

"That is a head-shy pony," Dr. Crandal said. "Don't become too attached to her, girls. Mr. Kennedy might decide to sell her for salvage."

"What's 'salvage'?" asked Anna.

"That's when horses are bought for their meat," Lulu told Anna.

Dr. Crandal left. But the Pony Pals stayed. "We have to make Beauty healthy and beautiful again," said Anna. "And find her a good home so Mr. Kennedy won't sell her for salvage."

"She's head-shy," said Pam. "We won't even be able to put a halter on her. No one will buy her for a pet."

"We'll figure it out," said Lulu.

"We *have* to help Beauty," said Anna.

Pam remembered the terrified look she'd

seen in Beauty's eyes when she touched her head. It was the most frightened look she'd ever seen in a pony. Maybe her father was right. Maybe Beauty was too scared and wild to be a pet. Maybe the Pony Pals wouldn't be able to save her.

Dear Mr. Kennedy

On Monday morning Pam left for school extra early. She carried oats and hay for Beauty in a shopping bag because her books were in her backpack.

Pam decided that if Beauty wasn't in the field, she'd leave the food for her on the rock. But Beauty was waiting for Pam in the field.

"Hi, Beauty," Pam called.

Beauty didn't run away when she saw Pam. Instead she trotted over to the flat rock and nickered as if to say, "Where's my oats?"

Pam held out a handful of oats mixed with vitamins. As Beauty ate from her hand, Pam told her, "I can't stay to groom you this morning. I have to go to school. But I'll be back later with Anna and Lulu." Beauty looked up at Pam and nickered as if to say, "Thank you." Pam patted the pony on the side and said good-bye.

At three o'clock the Pony Pals walked out of Wiggins Elementary together. "I bet Beauty will be waiting for us," said Lulu. "Let's hurry."

"I can't go today," said Anna. "I have my tutor for reading." She took the curry-combs and brushes out of her backpack and handed them to Lulu. "Tell Beauty hi for me," she said.

"Let's go Pam," said Lulu.

"Before we take care of Beauty, we have to go see Mrs. Baxter," said Pam. "We promised we'd let her know if we saw the pony again."

"*We* didn't promise," said Anna.

"But we have to tell her that Beauty is Mr. Kennedy's pony," said Pam. "And that we want to talk to Mr. Kennedy. We should tell him we're taking care of Beauty."

"I don't think we should talk to Mr. Kennedy yet," said Lulu. "The most important thing is to take care of Beauty."

"I want to talk to Mr. Kennedy *now,*" said Pam. "Beauty is his pony and he should know about her condition. Maybe he can tell us why she's so head shy. And I bet he'll want us to find her a good home."

"What if he tells us we can't take care of Beauty?" said Lulu. "A person who leaves a pony alone all winter could be mean enough to do that."

"I think he hired someone to take care of her and *they* didn't do the job," said Pam.

"I think he's mean and he just left his pony," said Lulu. "He might sell Beauty for salvage."

"I agree with Lulu," said Anna. "I think we should wait to talk to Mr. Kennedy."

"So it's two against one, Pam," said Lulu. "We don't tell Mrs. Baxter about Beauty until she's in good enough shape to be someone's pet. Come on, let's go. Beauty must be hungry."

Pam put her hands on her hips. "I don't care if it's two against one," she said. "I'm going to go to see Mrs. Baxter now. It's our responsibility to tell Beauty's owner that we found her."

"But we don't agree," said Lulu.

"Lightning and I found Beauty," said Pam. "So I get to say what we should do for her."

"*One* Pony Pal can't decide what to do," said Anna. "We *all* have to agree."

"I'm going to see Mrs. Baxter now. You can come if you want." Pam turned and headed toward Baxter Realty. Lulu and Anna did not follow her.

Mrs. Baxter was surprised that the neglected pony belonged to Mr. Kennedy. "I don't think he would leave an animal alone," Mrs. Baxter said. "Maybe someone was supposed to take care of the pony and didn't do *their* job."

"That's what I think," said Pam. "I want to talk to Mr. Kennedy and tell him the Pony Pals will take care of Beauty."

"Mr. Kennedy and I keep in touch by sending faxes," said Mrs. Baxter. "I'll write and tell him that you discovered his pony."

"Can I write the fax?" asked Pam.

"Sure," said Mrs. Baxter. Pam sat down to write it.

After she sent the fax, Pam went over to the Kennedy property. Lulu was taking burrs out of Beauty's tail.

"Hi, Beauty," Pam said. She didn't say hi to Lulu. And Lulu didn't say hi to her. Pam picked up a brush and worked on Beauty's coat.

After a while Lulu asked, "Did you talk to Mr. Kennedy?"

"No," answered Pam. "I sent him a fax. It's like a letter, only the person gets it right away."

"I know what a fax is," said Lulu. "Did Mrs. Baxter write it?"

"I wrote it," Pam said.

"How come you didn't wait for us to write it together?" asked Lulu. "That's what we usually do when we're working on a Pony Pal Problem."

"If you came with me you could have helped write it," Pam said angrily.

Lulu's voice was angry, too. "You're acting weird, Pam," she said "Weird and bossy."

"Well you are, too!" shouted Pam.

Beauty didn't like the shouting. She snorted, jumped away from them, and ran into the woods.

"See what you did," said Lulu.

"See what *you* did," said Pam.

The two girls didn't say another word to each other. Lulu packed up the grooming tools. Pam laid out some hay for Beauty. Then they both left. But not together.

The first thing Pam did when she got home was go around to Lightning's paddock. "Lightning, I'm home," she called. Lightning ran across the field to greet her. Pam put her arms around her pony's neck and gave her a hug. "I missed you today," she said. "My friends are acting so stubborn. I get along better with ponies than people."

Lightning whinnied softly as if to say, "Don't worry. Everything will be all right." Pam leaned her cheek against Lightning's neck and thought, How can the Pony Pals help Beauty if we are fighting with one another?

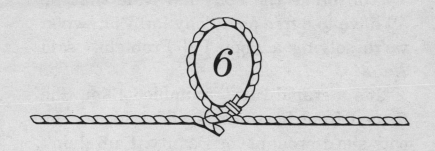

No Trespassing

The next morning Pam stopped at the Kennedy property to feed Beauty. Lulu and Anna were already there. "What are you doing here?" she asked them.

"Beauty is our pony, too," said Anna.

"But it's my job to take care of her in the morning. It's on my way to school," said Pam.

"Just because you saw her first you act like she's yours," said Lulu.

"Beauty is not mine and she's not yours," said Pam. "She's Mr. Kennedy's pony."

"You broke the Pony Pal Rule that we all have to agree on a Pony Pal Plan when we're solving a Pony Pal Problem," said Anna.

"It's a stupid rule," mumbled Pam. She turned from her friends and laid out the oats she'd brought for Beauty. Pam didn't say another word to Anna and Lulu.

Lulu put out a small pile of hay for the pony. She didn't speak, either.

Anna used the currycomb to brush mud off Beauty's side. Pam noticed that Anna was chewing her lower lip. She knew that was a sign that Anna was very angry.

I don't care if the whole world is angry at me, thought Pam. I'm doing what's best for Beauty.

Anna finally broke the silence. "What did you say in the fax to Mr. Kennedy?" she asked.

Pam pulled a folded piece of paper out of her pocket and held it out. Lulu took the fax and read it aloud.

Dear Mr. Kennedy:

I saw a pony on your property. She looks like she was on her own all winter. She is very skinny and her coat is all muddy. My friends and I are feeding and grooming her. We have our own ponies and know a lot about them. My father says it's your pony. He is a veterinarian and says that Beauty is undernourished, but not sick.

We would like to make Beauty beautiful again. We want to train her, too. Then we can find her a good home. It is hard to train Beauty because she is head shy and I can't put a halter on her. Do you know why she is head shy?

Thank you.

Sincerely,
Pam Crandal

PS
You can send me a fax at Baxter Realty.

When Lulu finished reading, Anna said, "That's not a very good letter."

"What's wrong with it?" asked Pam.

"You should have told Mr. Kennedy that you weren't trespassing on his property the first time you saw Beauty," said Lulu.

Pam knew Lulu was right. But she didn't say so.

"And you said you would find Beauty a good home," said Anna.

"What's wrong with that?" asked Pam.

"It sounds like you're going to give his pony away," said Anna. "You should have said that we would *sell* Beauty and give him the money. He'd like that better."

"You both think Mr. Kennedy is mean," said Pam. "I don't think he is. Today I'm going to see if he sent me an answer to the fax. If you want to come, you can."

Anna glared at Pam. "You're so bossy," she said.

The three girls walked to school in silence. Pam thought about how happy Mr. Kennedy would be that she found Beauty. If he offered her a reward she'd say, "My reward is to see that Beauty gets a good home."

After school Pam didn't wait to see if Lulu and Anna were going to Baxter Realty with her. They were still angry at her. And she was angry at them, too. So she was surprised when Anna and Lulu ran to catch up with her.

"We're going with you," Lulu told Pam.

"Beauty is our responsibility, too," said Anna.

"Do whatever you want," muttered Pam.

Pam saw Mr. Baxter sitting at the big desk near the office window. Her heart sank. Mr. Baxter didn't like the Pony Pals. He didn't like ponies, either.

The door to the office was open, so the Pony Pals walked in. Mr. Baxter looked up and growled, "What are you doing here?"

"Hello, Mr. Baxter," said Pam. "Did Mr. Kennedy send me a fax?"

"No. But he sent *me* one." Mr. Baxter scowled at the three girls. "Kennedy said you and your friends have been trespassing on his property." Mr. Baxter shook a finger at them. "You girls stay away from the

Kennedy place or you'll be in big trouble."

Pam didn't care if Mr. Baxter was acting mean, she had to know about Beauty. "Did Mr. Kennedy say anything about his pony?" she asked.

"He did," said Mr. Baxter.

The phone rang. Mr. Baxter turned his back on the girls to answer it.

Pam thought, Anna and Lulu were right. I should have waited to send Mr. Kennedy a fax. If we can't go on his land, how will we take care of Beauty? Pam felt so awful that she couldn't even look at Anna and Lulu.

When Mr. Baxter finished his phone call, he turned to the Pony Pals and said, "You still here?"

"What's going to happen to Mr. Kennedy's pony?" asked Anna.

Mr. Baxter snapped, "It's not your concern. And keep off Kennedy's property."

Pam ran out of the office ahead of Anna and Lulu. She didn't want Mr. Baxter to see her crying.

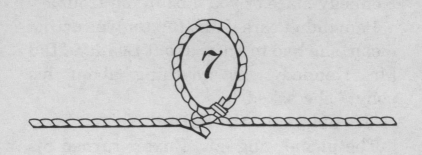

On the Fence

Anna and Lulu caught up with Pam. "I ruined everything," Pam cried. She wiped away tears with her fingers. "I'm sorry."

"Don't cry," said Anna. "It's not all your fault. Mr. Kennedy is a mean man."

"And Mr. Baxter made things even worse," said Lulu.

The three girls sat on a log by the side of the road to talk.

"What will we do now?" asked Pam.

"The important thing is to help Beauty," said Anna.

"Mr. Baxter wouldn't even tell us what's going to happen to her," Pam said.

"Or why Mr. Kennedy left her alone in the first place," said Anna.

"I know everything," said Lulu. "I saw the fax from Mr. Kennedy on Mr. Baxter's desk. I read it while he was on the phone."

"What did it say?" Anna asked.

"The R.C. Horse Auctions Company was going to pick up Beauty. They were supposed to sell her for Mr. Kennedy. But when they tried to halter her she hit her head on a tree and fell."

"That's probably why she's head shy!" exclaimed Anna.

"Beauty ran away from the men before they could catch her," said Lulu. "The auction company wrote Mr. Kennedy a letter, but he never received it. Mr. Kennedy called the auction company after he got Pam's fax. He told them to catch Beauty and sell her for salvage. They're picking her up on Saturday."

"Maybe someone will buy her for a pet at the auction," said Anna.

"No one will buy a skinny, head-shy pony as a pet," said Lulu.

"Which means she will be sold for salvage," said Pam.

"Oh, no!" cried Anna. "We can't let that happen to Beauty."

"It's all my fault," said Pam. "I shouldn't have sent that fax. You were right."

"Forget that," Lulu told Pam. "We have to think about helping Beauty."

"We have to work together to figure out what to do next," Anna said.

"And we have to find a way to still take care of Beauty," said Lulu.

"How can we take care of her if we can't go near her?" asked Pam. "It'd be trespassing again. We'd get into so much trouble."

"If we can't go to her, she'll have to come to us," Lulu said. "Who owns the land next to the Kennedy place?"

"Let me think," said Pam. Pam took out a notebook and drew a map.

She talked as she drew. "The Martins own the fields next to Kennedy's woods. And the Nelson farm is on the other side. I don't know whose land goes behind it."

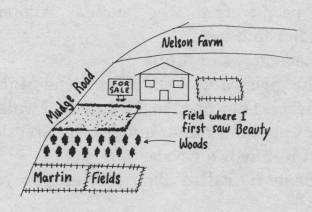

"Where can we go so Beauty will find us?" asked Anna.

Lulu pointed to the fence line between the Martins' property and Mr. Kennedy's woods. "I think we should go there," she said.

"The Martins gave us permission to go in their fields anytime we want," said Pam. "So we won't be trespassing."

"Beauty is always hiding in those woods," said Anna. "That's probably why the people from the auction company couldn't find her."

"Let's go," said Lulu.

The girls ran all the way to the Martin property. They opened the gate and walked over to the fence that divided the first field from Kennedy's woods.

"Beauty!" called Pam. "Come get your oats."

"Beauty!" shouted Lulu. "We're over here."

"I have an apple for you!" yelled Pam.

Soon the girls heard the sound of pounding hooves. Beauty was coming toward them from the woods. She ran over to the apple that Pam held out for her.

"See how sweet and smart she is," said Anna.

"But she's still so skinny," said Pam.

"And her coat needs a lot more work," said Lulu. She held out a handful of oats through the fence rails. Pam sat on the fence and patted Beauty's side. Beauty nickered as if to say, "I have good oats and good friends."

"Beauty isn't afraid of us anymore," said Lulu. "If we can train her before the auction, someone might still buy her for a pet."

"Maybe she won't be head shy today," said Pam. She reached out toward Beauty's head. Beauty saw the hand coming, turned, and charged back into the woods.

"She's still head shy," said Pam sadly. "No one will buy her for a pet if she acts like that."

"What are we going to do?" asked Anna.

"Let's come up with three ideas," said Lulu, "and meet at the diner before school tomorrow."

Anna and Lulu knew Pam still felt badly about the fax and their fight. Anna put her arm around Pam's shoulder. "Don't worry," she said.

"The Pony Pals have solved some tough problems before," said Lulu. "We'll solve this one."

"We're friends," said Anna. "Best friends. And we'll do the best we can for Beauty."

The Pony Pals walked across the field together. Pam was thinking, What if our best isn't enough to save Beauty?

Three Ideas

Pam made two stops on the way to school the next morning. The first one was to feed Beauty. The second stop was at Off-Main Diner where she met Anna and Lulu for a Pony Pal meeting. Anna and Lulu were already in the booth. Pam slid in next to Anna. Lulu handed her a glass of milk and a muffin.

"Who's going first?" asked Anna.

"I will," Lulu said. She read her idea out loud.

Find a buyer for Beauty <u>BEFORE</u> Mr. Kennedy sends her back to the auction.

"That's a good idea," said Anna. "And it works great with my idea." She put a drawing out on the table.

"I think Ms. Wiggins should buy Beauty," said Anna.

"She misses her old pony, Winston," said Lulu. "It's so sad when your pony dies."

"Her horse, Picasso, misses Winston,

too," said Pam. "Beauty could be a stable-mate for Picasso."

"Ms. Wiggins loves driving," said Anna. "Beauty is a Morgan. And Morgans are great driving ponies."

"But Beauty is head shy," Lulu pointed out. "We can't even halter her. How can she be a driving pony?"

"My mom gave me a lesson last night on how to get a pony over being head shy," said Pam. "I'll work with her this afternoon."

"How can you work with her if there's a fence between you and Beauty?" asked Lulu.

"My idea will solve that problem," said Pam. She read her idea to Anna and Lulu.

Open the gate between the Martin and Kennedy properties. Then Beauty can come to us.

"I didn't know there was a gate in that fence," said Anna.

"It's at the other end," said Pam.

The Pony Pals finished eating and then walked to school.

That afternoon the Pony Pals found Beauty waiting for them at the fence. They opened the gate. Lulu put out Beauty's oats and hay in the Martins' field. Beauty ran through the gate and over to the food. After she finished eating, the Pony Pals groomed her.

Pam concentrated on brushing the pony's strong neck. "I'm going to work close to her head," Pam told Anna and Lulu. "I'll slowly move from her neck to her head. Then maybe she'll let me brush her face. You keep grooming her sides."

Pam gently touched the back of Beauty's head. She quickly took her hand away and went back to brushing Beauty's neck. The pony looked at Pam and nickered as if to say, "What do you think you're doing?" But Beauty's eyes weren't frightened. And she didn't run away.

"Good pony," said Pam. Then she touched the pony's cheek several times. Each time she kept her hand on Beauty's face a little longer. She spoke soothingly to the pony the whole time.

"She trusts you," said Anna.

"I'm going to try touching her from the front now," Pam said. She faced Beauty and touched her under the chin. Then she began touching her around the nose and forehead.

"It's working," said Lulu.

"Now for the big test," said Pam. "Hand me a halter."

Lulu took a halter out of her backpack and handed it to Pam. When Beauty saw the halter, she snorted and jumped back. Pam tried to halter Beauty again. This time the pony shook her head and ran a few yards off. She whinnied at the girls as if to say, "I thought you were my friends."

"I'm doing this for your own good, Beauty," said Pam. "I wouldn't hurt you." But the pony did not understand.

"No one wants a pony that can't be haltered," said Anna sadly.

"We only have two days until the auction," said Lulu.

Pam shook her head. "We have to save Beauty. We just have to!"

Friends

Walking home along Riddle Road, Pam wondered how she could train Beauty in two days. By the time she got home she knew what to do. She ran out to Lightning's paddock. "Lightning, I have an important job for you," she told her pony. Then she went into the house and phoned Lulu.

"I think Lightning can help us with Beauty," Pam told Lulu. "Beauty loved being near Lightning before."

"Maybe she won't be so scared when we try to put a halter on her," Lulu said.

Next, Pam called Anna to see if she agreed with the plan. "Lightning is the perfect teacher for Beauty," said Anna.

Pam remembered Anna's idea that Ms. Wiggins should buy Beauty to replace Winston. "Have you asked Ms. Wiggins yet?" Pam asked.

"Yes," said Anna. "I told her I had something important to talk to her about. I'm meeting her at the diner after school tomorrow."

"Good," said Pam.

After school the next day, Pam went home, saddled up Lightning, and rode her down Mudge Road. They met Lulu near the Martin property. Pam dismounted and led Lightning into the field. Beauty was waiting for them by the gate. When she saw Lightning, she whinnied a hello. Lightning whinnied back to her.

Lulu opened the gate and Beauty came over to Lightning. Pam held a halter and lead rope behind her back so the head shy pony wouldn't see it. Beauty was so interested in Lightning that she didn't notice or care when Pam slipped the halter on her. Lulu held out a handful of oats for each of the ponies. While Beauty ate, Pam buckled the halter.

"We did it!" Pam said. "It worked."

Next, Lulu led Lightning in front of Beauty. "Okay, Beauty," Pam said. "We're going to follow Lightning and Lulu." Pam held on to Beauty's lead rope as she walked behind her pony and Lulu. Beauty walked on beside Pam. She was happy to be following Lightning and Lulu in a big circle around the field. "Thanks, Lightning," Pam called to her own pony. "You're a wonderful teacher."

Lightning nickered as if to say, "What did you expect?"

After they'd led the ponies around the field three times, Pam said, "Let's groom Beauty. She still looks dirty."

"Maybe she'll let us work on the top of her mane today," said Lulu. "It's a mess."

Pam noticed a red car coming along Mudge Road. It slowed down and stopped.

"I hope that's not Mr. Kennedy or Mr. Baxter," said Lulu.

"Me too," said Pam. But it was Ms. Wiggins and Anna who stepped out of the car.

"I wish we had time to groom Beauty before Ms. Wiggins saw her," said Pam. She patted the pony on the neck. "Well, at least you have on a halter," she told her. "Now behave yourself for Ms. Wiggins. You could have a wonderful life on the Wiggins estate."

But Ms. Wiggins didn't come to the field to see Beauty. Instead, she leaned on the fence and motioned for Lulu and Pam to come over to her and Anna. Lulu and Pam unhitched the lead ropes from the ponies' halters and ran up to the fence to talk to Ms. Wiggins.

"That's Beauty, Ms. Wiggins," said Lulu. "She'll be really beautiful when we groom her more. She needs to put on some weight, too."

"And she's a Morgan," said Pam. "Morgans are great driving ponies."

Ms. Wiggins didn't look at Beauty and she seemed sad. "I'm sure the pony you found is wonderful, girls," Ms. Wiggins said. "But I'm not ready to have another pony. I came here to tell you that myself. No one can replace Winston. Not right now."

Pam could understand how Ms. Wiggins felt.

"Winston was a very special pony," said Anna.

"I knew that the Pony Pals would understand," said Ms. Wiggins. And then she left.

"What do we do now?" asked Anna.

"Make Beauty the best-looking, best-behaved pony we can," said Pam. "Then maybe someone will buy her for a pet at the auction instead of for salvage."

"But the auction people are coming for

her tomorrow," said Lulu. "We can't turn Beauty into a perfect pony by then."

"But we have to try," said Pam.

The Pony Pals took turns leading Beauty around the field so she'd become used to different people leading her. She was very well-behaved for that. But when Pam tried to put a saddle on Beauty's back, she bucked and scooted to the side. It took two carrots to calm her down.

"She's still a wild pony," said Anna sadly.

"We should have put something light on her back first," said Pam. "Tomorrow we'll start with a saddle blanket."

"Tomorrow the auction company is taking Beauty away," said Lulu.

"We'll work with her until the last minute," said Pam. "And I want to be here when they take her away."

"Are we going to help them catch her?" asked Anna.

"Maybe we should," said Lulu, "so she won't be too upset."

Beauty lowered her head and nudged

Pam's pocket to check for more carrots. "No more today," Pam said. She put her arms around Beauty's neck and leaned her cheek against her. Tears filled Pam's eyes. Would the next day be the last day of Beauty's life?

The Meeting

Early the next morning, the Pony Pals went to the Martins' fields. Beauty was waiting for them at the gate. They put Lightning in the first field and Snow White and Acorn in the second field.

Lulu fed Beauty. Next, Pam and Lightning gave her a half-hour lesson on the lead rope. After the lesson, while Pam and Lulu brushed and rubbed Beauty's coat, Anna combed her mane and tail.

"She's shed most of her winter coat,"

said Pam. "Look how shiny she is underneath."

"And she's already gaining weight," said Lulu.

"She's beginning to look beautiful," said Anna.

"If only we had more time to train her," said Pam. "I know we could make her into a pony someone would want for a pet."

Pam noticed a horse and rider coming along Mudge Road. "Look. There's Ms. Wiggins and Picasso," said Anna.

"I wonder why she's here," said Lulu.

Ms. Wiggins tied Picasso's lead rope to a fence post. Then she came through the gate and walked over to the Pony Pals and Beauty.

"I've been thinking," she told them. "I'm not ready for another pony, but Picasso is very lonely without a stablemate. So I have come to take a look at Mr. Kennedy's pony." Ms. Wiggins walked around Beauty. "She's well-built and has a sturdy frame," she told the girls. "She's thin. But a healthy diet would change that." Next, Ms. Wiggins walked in front of Beauty. "She has a sweet face and nice eyes," she said.

"Beauty's a great pony," said Pam. "She needs more training because she was alone for a long time. But she can be wonderful. I know she can."

Ms. Wiggins reached up to pat the pony on the cheek. Beauty threw back her head and backed up. "Is she head shy?" asked Ms. Wiggins. Lulu said that she was. And Pam told Ms. Wiggins how Beauty hit her head when the auction company came to pick her up.

"Some horses never get over a bad experience like that," said Ms. Wiggins. "I wanted to give the pony a home and Picasso a stablemate. But Beauty may be too wild."

A horn honked. A horse trailer pulled up along the side of the road. Pam saw R.C. Horse Auctions in red letters on the side of the trailer.

"They're here to pick up Beauty," Pam told Ms. Wiggins. "They're going to sell her for salvage at an auction."

"Look," Anna said. The girls and Ms. Wiggins looked to where Anna pointed. Beauty was walking toward Picasso. The big horse watched the bold pony. Beauty nickered. Picasso reached his head over the fence and sniffed at Beauty's face. Beauty squealed happily. Picasso whinnied softly. The pony and the horse sniffed each other's face. Then they rubbed cheeks.

"I've never seen him do that with a strange horse," said Ms. Wiggins. "He likes her."

"They're so cute together," said Anna.

"Picasso must be so lonely without Winston," added Lulu.

"Come on, girls," said Ms. Wiggins. "We don't want those men coming in the field and frightening Beauty again."

Ms. Wiggins and the Pony Pals ran across the field. Two men were getting out of the trailer. One of them was carrying a

long coil of rope. The other held a narrow canvas bag. Pam wondered if there was a gun in the bag.

"Hello," Ms. Wiggins said to the men. "I'm Wilhelmina Wiggins."

"I'm Ron Crew," the red-haired man said. "R.C. Horse Auctions is my business."

"Mr. Crew, I'd like to talk to you about buying the pony you've come to pick up," said Ms. Wiggins.

"Mr. Kennedy gave orders to catch that pony and sell her at auction," Mr. Crew said. "She won't get away this time."

"Did Mr. Kennedy tell you how much he wanted for his pony?" asked Ms. Wiggins.

"He said she was ruined," said Mr. Crew. "We're going to sell her for meat. Today, that's thirty-five cents a pound." He turned to the other man. "Let's go, Joe. The auction is at three o'clock."

Ms. Wiggins looked over to Picasso and Beauty. They were still rubbing faces. "Wait!" Ms. Wiggins told the two men. "I'll give you forty cents a pound for that pony. That should satisfy Mr. Kennedy."

"You're going to pay forty cents a pound for that wild pony?" Ron Crew said.

"Yes, I am," Ms. Wiggins said.

Ms. Wiggins took a checkbook and pen out of her pocket. She made out a check and handed it to Mr. Crew.

"Let's go, Joe," he said to his helper.

The two men got into the trailer and drove away without Beauty.

"Well, girls," Ms. Wiggins said, "will you help me bring my new pony home?"

The Pony Pals shrieked, "Yes!" and hit high fives.

"Is Beauty tame enough for us to pony her back to my place?" Ms. Wiggins asked the three girls.

"She'll follow Lightning," said Pam.

"And she'll definitely follow Picasso," added Anna with a grin.

"Then saddle up and let's go," said Ms. Wiggins.

Pam ran back into the field calling, "Lightning, come here." Lightning ran over to her. Pam gave her pony a big kiss on the cheek. "You found a wonderful wild pony," said Pam. "Now you're going to help bring her to a new home."

Dear Reader:

I am having a lot of fun researching and writing books about the Pony Pals. I've met many interesting kids and adults who love ponies. And I've visited some wonderful ponies at homes, farms, and riding schools.

Before writing Pony Pals I wrote fourteen novels for children and young adults. Four of these were honored by Children's Choice Awards.

I live in Sharon, Connecticut, with my husband, Lee, and our dog, Willie. Our daughter is all grown up and has her own apartment in New York City.

Besides writing novels I like to draw, paint, garden, and swim. I didn't have a pony when I was growing up, but I have always loved them and dreamt about riding. Now I take riding lessons on a horse named Saz.

I like reading and writing about ponies as much as I do riding. Which proves to me that you don't have to ride a pony to love them. And you certainly don't need a pony to be a Pony Pal.

Happy Reading,

Jeanne Betancourt

Pony Pals

Be a Pony Pal!

❏ BBC0-590-48583-0	#1	I Want a Pony	$2.99
❏ BBC0-590-48584-9	#2	A Pony for Keeps	$2.99
❏ BBC0-590-48585-7	#3	A Pony in Trouble	$2.99
❏ BBC0-590-48586-5	#4	Give Me Back My Pony	$2.99
❏ BBC0-590-25244-5	#5	Pony to the Rescue	$2.99
❏ BBC0-590-25245-3	#6	Too Many Ponies	$2.99
❏ BBC0-590-54338-5	#7	Runaway Pony	$2.99
❏ BBC0-590-54339-3	#8	Good-bye Pony	$2.99
❏ BBC0-590-62974-3	#9	The Wild Pony	$2.99
❏ BBC0-590-62975-1	#10	Don't Hurt My Pony	$2.99
❏ BBC0-590-86597-8	#11	Circus Pony	$2.99
❏ BBC0-590-86598-6	#12	Keep Out, Pony!	$2.99
❏ BBC0-590-86600-1	#13	The Girl Who Hated Ponies	$2.99
❏ BBC0-590-86601-X	#14	Pony-Sitters	$3.50
❏ BBC0-590-86632-X	#15	The Blind Pony	$3.50
❏ BBC0-590-37459-1	#16	The Missing Pony Pal	$3.50
❏ BBC0-590-37460-5	#17	Detective Pony	$3.50
❏ BBC0-590-51295-1	#18	The Saddest Pony	$3.50
❏ BBC0-590-63397-X	#19	Moving Pony	$3.50
❏ BBC0-590-63401-1	#20	Stolen Ponies	$3.50
❏ BBC0-590-63405-4	#21	The Winning Pony	$3.50
❏ BBC0-590-74210-8		Pony Pals Super Special #1: The Baby Pony	$5.99
❏ BBC0-590-86631-1		Pony Pals Super Special #2: The Lives of our Ponies	$5.99
❏ BBC0-590-37461-3		Pony Pals Super Special #3: The Ghost Pony	$5.99

Available wherever you buy books, or use this order form.

Send orders to Scholastic Inc., P.O. Box 7500, Jefferson City, MO 65102

Please send me the books I have checked above. I am enclosing $_____ (please add $2.00 to cover shipping and handling). Send check or money order — no cash or C.O.D.s please.

Please allow four to six weeks for delivery. Offer good in the U.S.A. only. Sorry, mail orders are not available to residents of Canada. Prices subject to change.

Name_____ Birthdate ____/____/____
     First   Last   M   D   Y

Address_____

City_____ State_____ Zip_____

Telephone (_____)_____ ❏ Boy   ❏ Girl

Where did you buy this book? ❏ Bookstore   ❏ Book Fair   ❏ Book Club   ❏ Other   PP399